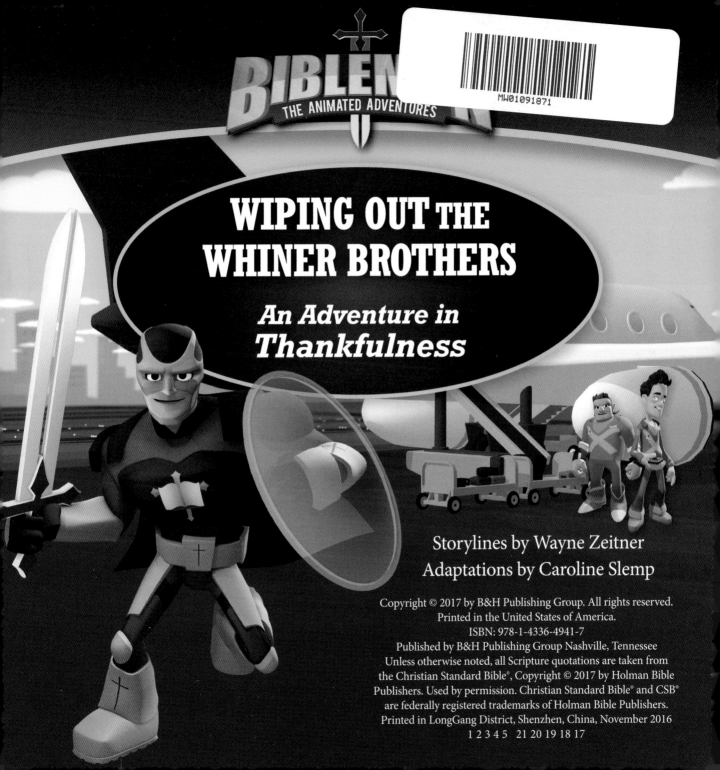

BIBLEMAN
THE ANIMATED ADVENTURES

WIPING OUT THE WHINER BROTHERS

An Adventure in Thankfulness

Storylines by Wayne Zeitner
Adaptations by Caroline Slemp

Copyright © 2017 by B&H Publishing Group. All rights reserved.
Printed in the United States of America.
ISBN: 978-1-4336-4941-7
Published by B&H Publishing Group Nashville, Tennessee
Unless otherwise noted, all Scripture quotations are taken from
the Christian Standard Bible®, Copyright © 2017 by Holman Bible
Publishers. Used by permission. Christian Standard Bible® and CSB®
are federally registered trademarks of Holman Bible Publishers.
Printed in LongGang District, Shenzhen, China, November 2016
1 2 3 4 5   21 20 19 18 17

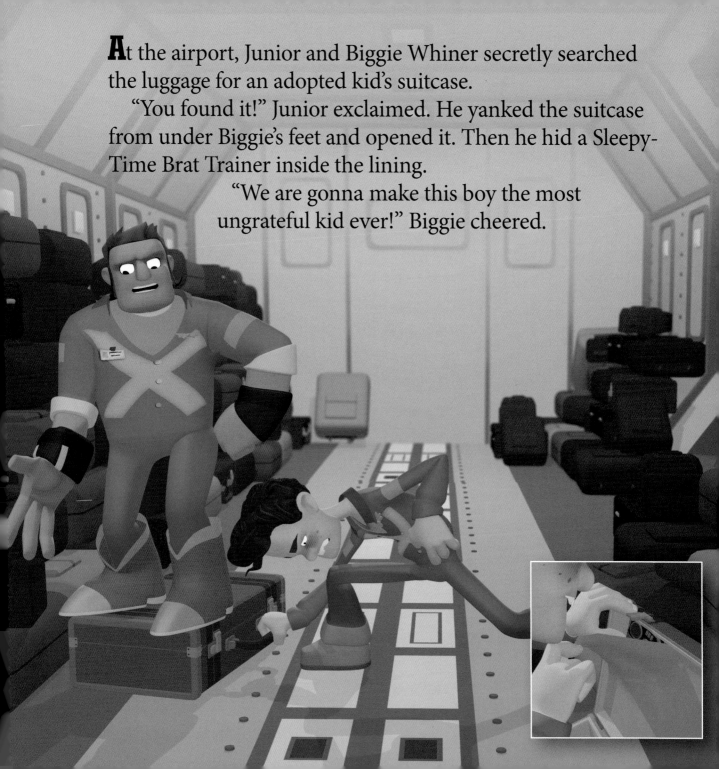

At the airport, Junior and Biggie Whiner secretly searched the luggage for an adopted kid's suitcase.

"You found it!" Junior exclaimed. He yanked the suitcase from under Biggie's feet and opened it. Then he hid a Sleepy-Time Brat Trainer inside the lining.

"We are gonna make this boy the most ungrateful kid ever!" Biggie cheered.

Bibleman was waiting for Aroad at the plane's exit. "Aroad! Welcome to America!" Bibleman said, taking Aroad's suitcase from the cart. "Your new foster parents have been so excited for you to come."

Aroad smiled from ear to ear. "I bet not as excited as me!"

They headed for the Biblecycle and left for Aroad's new home.

Mr. and Mrs. Clarke greeted Bibleman and Aroad at the door of their home.

"We've been expecting you!" they exclaimed.

"Hello! This is Aroad," Bibleman said.

"Welcome, Aroad," Mrs. Clarke said. "We're so happy to meet you. Let's go inside to see your new room."

"Thank you all. God has really blessed me today," Aroad said.

After Bibleman left, Mr. and Mrs. Clarke tucked Aroad into bed and said good night.

As soon as Aroad fell asleep, the Sleepy-Time Brat Trainer turned on and played a recording of Junior and Biggie's voices: "This bed is too lumpy. This house is too cold. I wish I were back at my real home." The recording repeated and played all night long.

The next morning, Aroad woke up grumpy. He went downstairs and saw that Mr. and Mrs. Clarke had made a big breakfast.

"Good morning," Mrs. Clarke said. "Did you sleep well?"

"No," Aroad replied. "My bed was too lumpy, and it was too cold. I don't want this food . . . and I want to go home!" Aroad stormed off.

The projection screen at the Bibleteam headquarters began flashing.

Melody checked it out. "Threat level seven coming from the Clarke residence."

"Aroad must be in danger," Bibleman said. "Cypher, you're with me. Biblegirl and Melody, continue to monitor here."

When Bibleman and Cypher arrived at the house, Cypher studied his tablet.

"There's a signal coming from this suitcase." Cypher reached in the suitcase and pulled out the Brat Trainer. "Bingo. It has a tracking signal, . . . and it's making noise. This must be a sleep learning tool," Cypher explained. "It plays phrases while people sleep to leave an impression on them when they wake up."

"Aroad," Bibleman said, "let's talk about thankfulness. In Luke 17, we learn about ten lepers. One day, Jesus walked by them, and the sick men shouted, 'Jesus, have mercy on us!' 'Show yourselves to the priests,' Jesus said."

"They obeyed and were healed! But, only one of them ran back to thank Jesus. He understood 1 Thessalonians 5:18," Bibleman finished.

"Give thanks in everything," Aroad recited, "for this is God's will for you in Christ Jesus."

"Welcome back, my friend," Bibleman said.

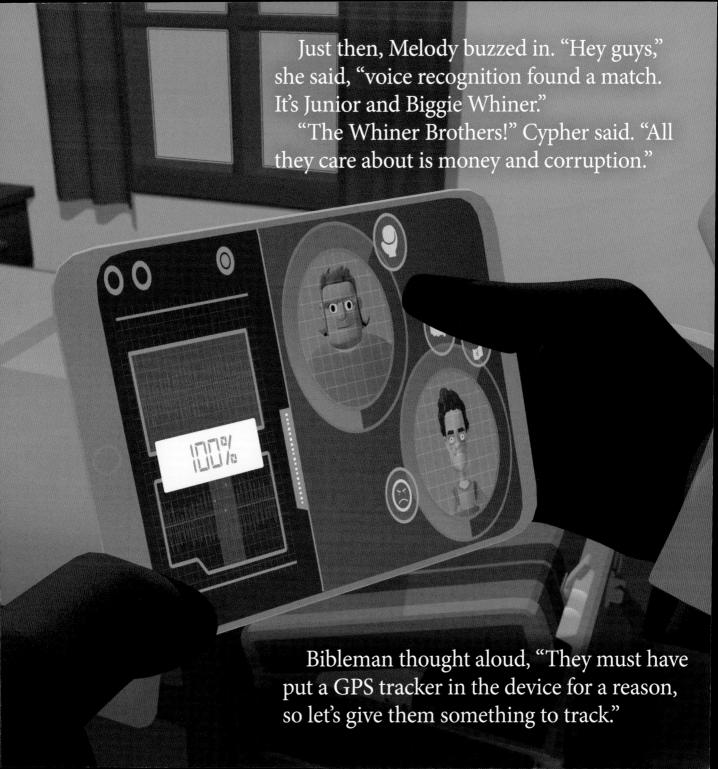

Just then, Melody buzzed in. "Hey guys," she said, "voice recognition found a match. It's Junior and Biggie Whiner."

"The Whiner Brothers!" Cypher said. "All they care about is money and corruption."

Bibleman thought aloud, "They must have put a GPS tracker in the device for a reason, so let's give them something to track."

Junior cheered, "They've taken the bait! We'll track Bibleman and discover where headquarters is. Every villain will pay us top dollar to learn the location. We'll be filthy rich!"

Biggie studied the map on his tablet and said, "The signal is coming from there!" He pointed to a row of buildings, and Junior pulled into the parking lot.

Following the signal, Junior and Biggie found themselves in a dark building. The tablet's tracker flashed red.

"The Brat Trainer must be right here!" Junior felt around and picked it up. "Wait, it's playing . . . Scripture!"

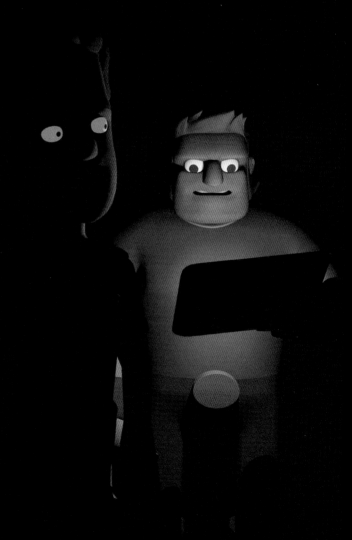

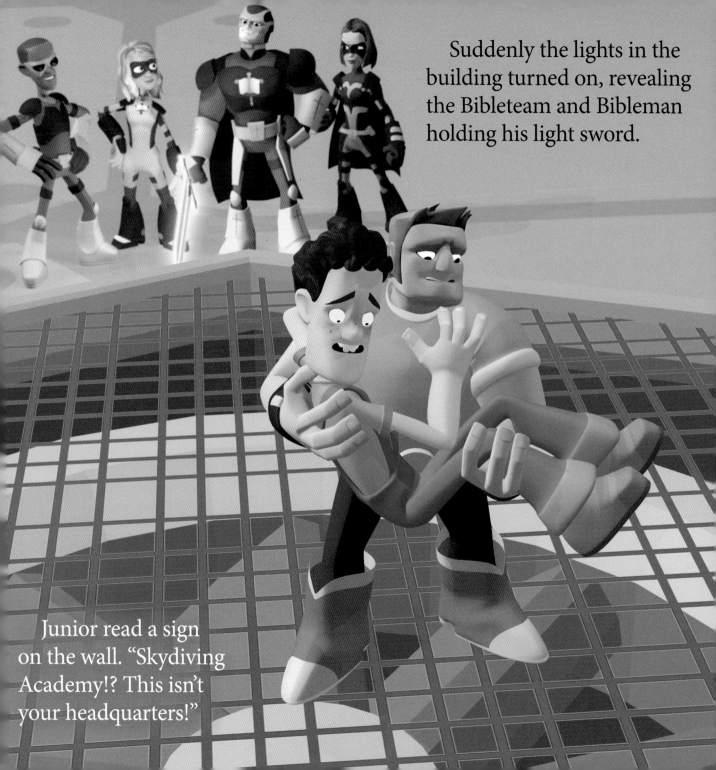

Suddenly the lights in the building turned on, revealing the Bibleteam and Bibleman holding his light sword.

Junior read a sign on the wall. "Skydiving Academy!? This isn't your headquarters!"

"Uh, Junior?" Biggie looked down. The brothers were standing above a huge propeller, which began to spin.

Bibleman recited 1 Thessalonians 5:18, pointed his sword at the fan, and shot an energy bolt at it. The fan spun faster and faster until it rocketed Biggie and Junior right through the roof.

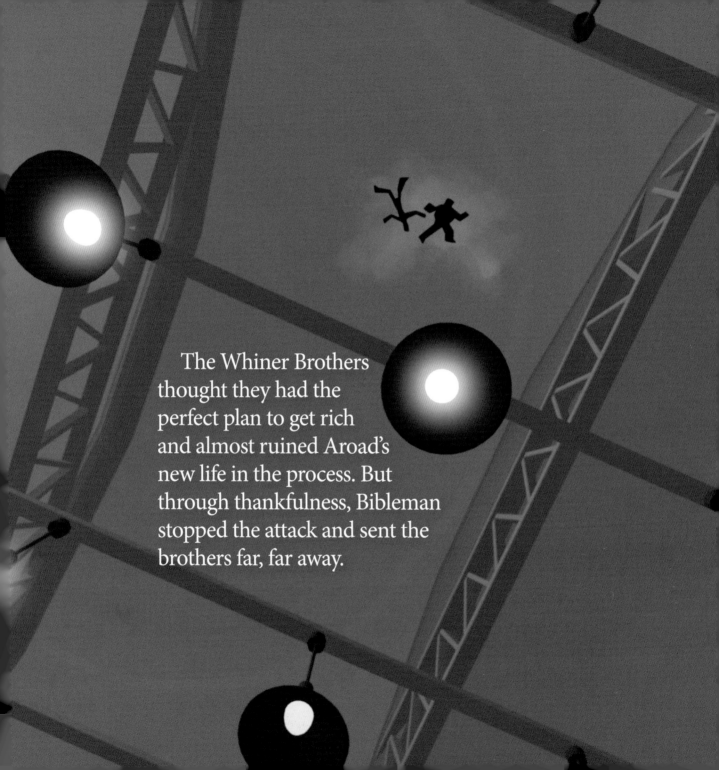

The Whiner Brothers
thought they had the
perfect plan to get rich
and almost ruined Aroad's
new life in the process. But
through thankfulness, Bibleman
stopped the attack and sent the
brothers far, far away.

Although the Ambassador lured kids into foolishness, the Bibleteam helped us all realize that by obeying God's Word we will become strong, wise, and covered by His grace.

Then Bibleman fired a stream of energy from the sword, super-charging the belt and launching the Ambassador into the air.

Bibleman aimed his sword at the conveyor belt. "For it is God's will that you silence the ignorance of foolish people by doing good!" Bibleman said. "That's 1 Peter 2:15!"

The Ambassador fell out of the truck's cabin door and onto the rock conveyor belt. He turned around to find Bibleman.

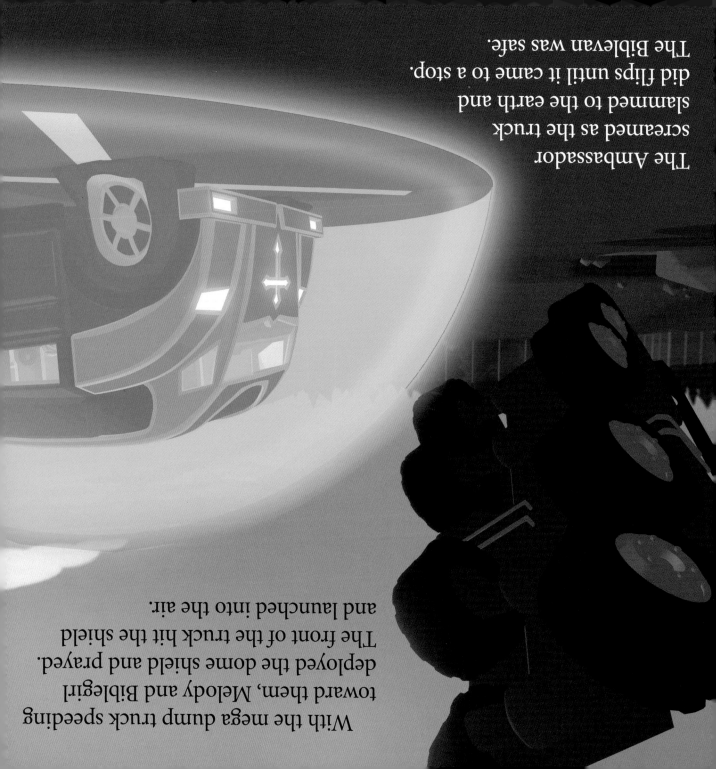

The Ambassador screamed as the truck slammed to the earth and did flips until it came to a stop. The Biblevan was safe.

With the mega dump truck speeding toward them, Melody and Biblegirl deployed the dome shield and prayed. The front of the truck hit the shield and launched into the air.

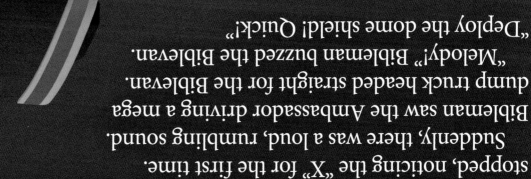

"I will call your attention to the giant 'X' your Biblevan landed on," the Ambassador said. Bibleman looked at the ground where the Biblevan had stopped, noticing the "X" for the first time.

Suddenly, there was a loud, rumbling sound. Bibleman saw the Ambassador driving a mega dump truck headed straight for the Biblevan.

"Melody!" Bibleman buzzed the Biblevan. "Deploy the dome shield! Quick!"

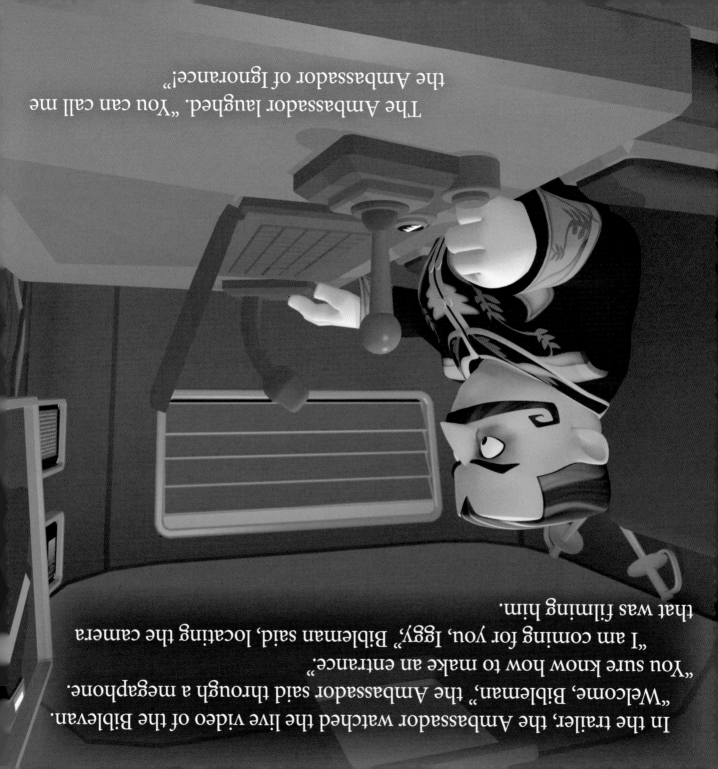

In the trailer, the Ambassador watched the live video of the Biblevan.

"Welcome, Bibleman," the Ambassador said through a megaphone. "You sure know how to make an entrance."

"I am coming for you, Iggy," Bibleman said, locating the camera that was filming him.

The Ambassador laughed. "You can call me the Ambassador of Ignorance!"

Just as the Biblevan passed through the gate, a row of metal spikes jutted out from the ground and popped the Biblevan's tires. The Biblevan slowed to a halt.

"You two stay in the van," Bibleman instructed. "I'm going to check things out."

When the Biblevan drove up to the quarry, the trio found a bulls-eye hanging from a tall gate. "That might mean the fence is electrified," Biblegirl said.

"If we're moving fast enough, it shouldn't matter," Bibleman floored the accelerator, launching the Biblevan at the gate.

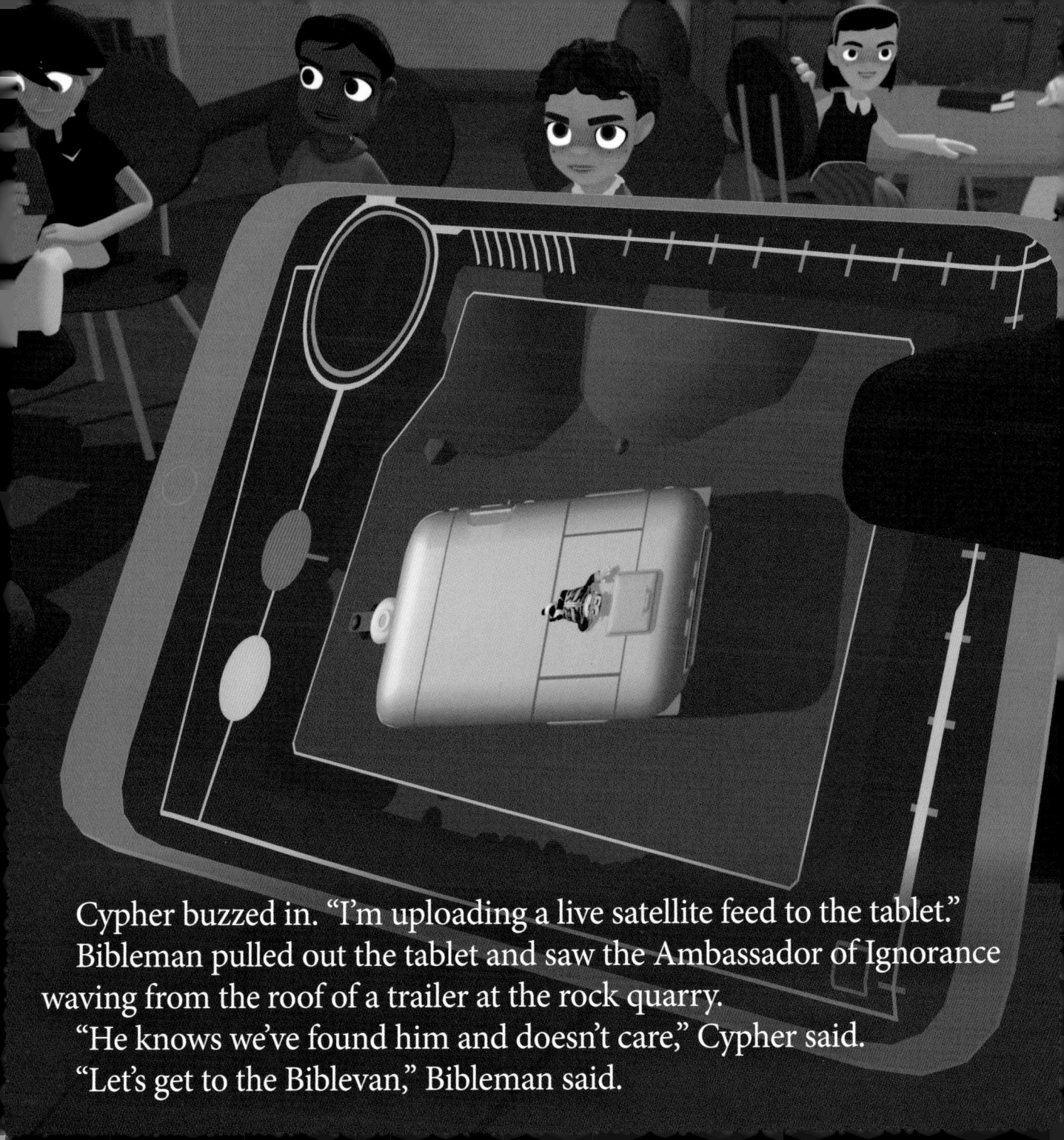

Cypher buzzed in. "I'm uploading a live satellite feed to the tablet."
Bibleman pulled out the tablet and saw the Ambassador of Ignorance
waving from the roof of a trailer at the rock quarry.

"He knows we've found him and doesn't care," Cypher said.

"Let's get to the Biblevan," Bibleman said.

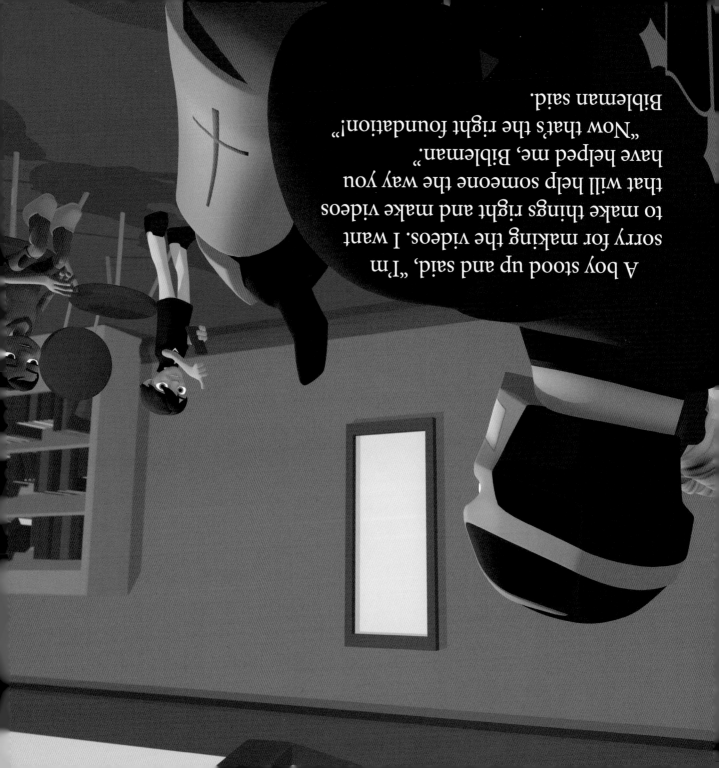

A boy stood up and said, "I'm sorry for making the videos. I want to make things right and make videos that will help someone the way you have helped me, Bibleman."

"Now that's the right foundation!" Bibleman said.

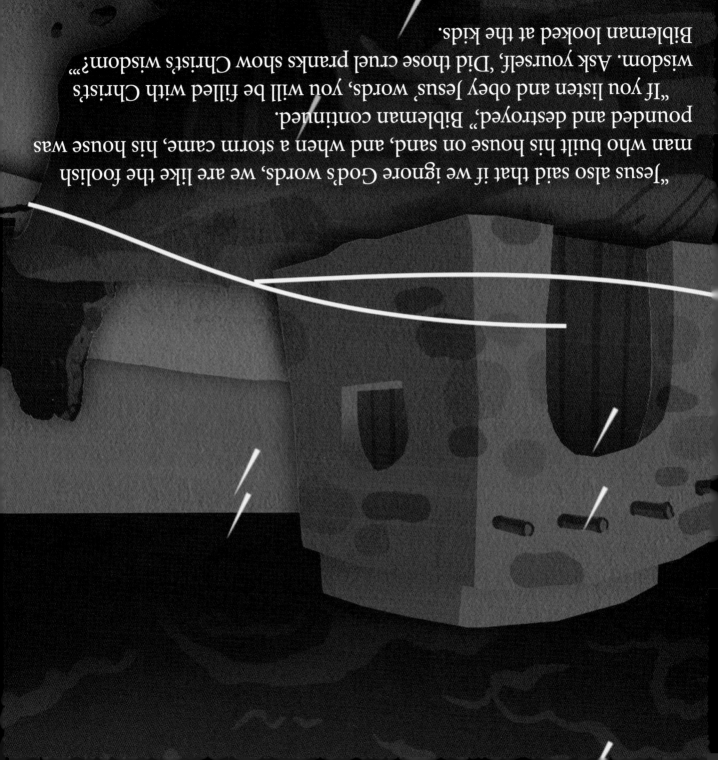

"Jesus also said that if we ignore God's words, we are like the foolish man who built his house on sand, and when a storm came, his house was pounded and destroyed," Bibleman continued.

"If you listen and obey Jesus' words, you will be filled with Christ's wisdom. Ask yourself, 'Did those cruel pranks show Christ's wisdom?'"

Bibleman looked at the kids.

In the youth room, Pastor Roberts introduced Bibleman, who took the stage.

Bibleman began, "Jesus told stories of wise and foolish people. In Matthew 7:24–27, Jesus said, if we hear His words and obey Him, then we are like the wise man who built his house on a foundation made of rock, because he knew life wouldn't always be sunny."

From his hideout, the Ambassador of Ignorance watched a surveillance video of the church. He saw a group of kids and their parents mingling outside. The Biblevan drove into view and parked.

"Wait a minute," he said. "Those are all my video brats! Bibleman! Already!?" the Ambassador exclaimed. "Well, he hasn't found me yet, but I guarantee he will come looking! HAHAHA!"

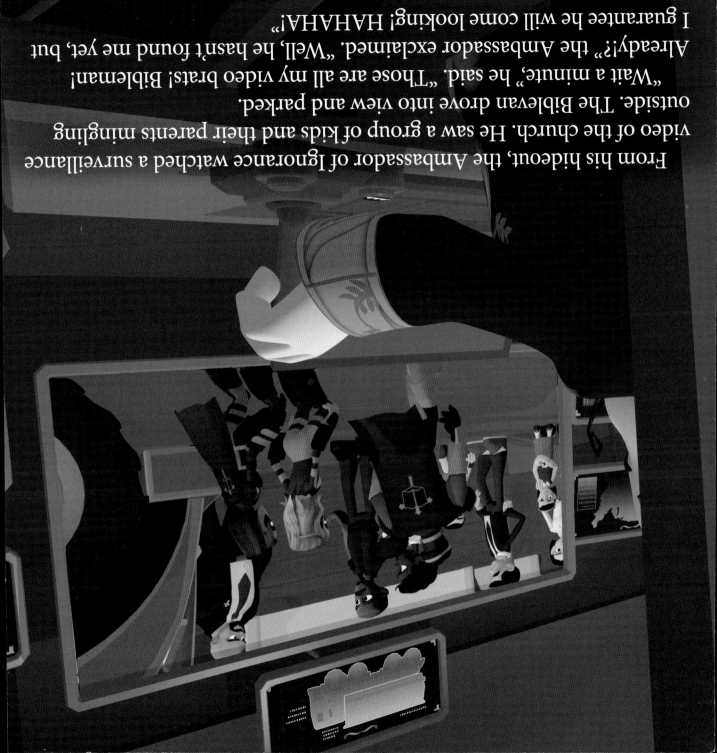

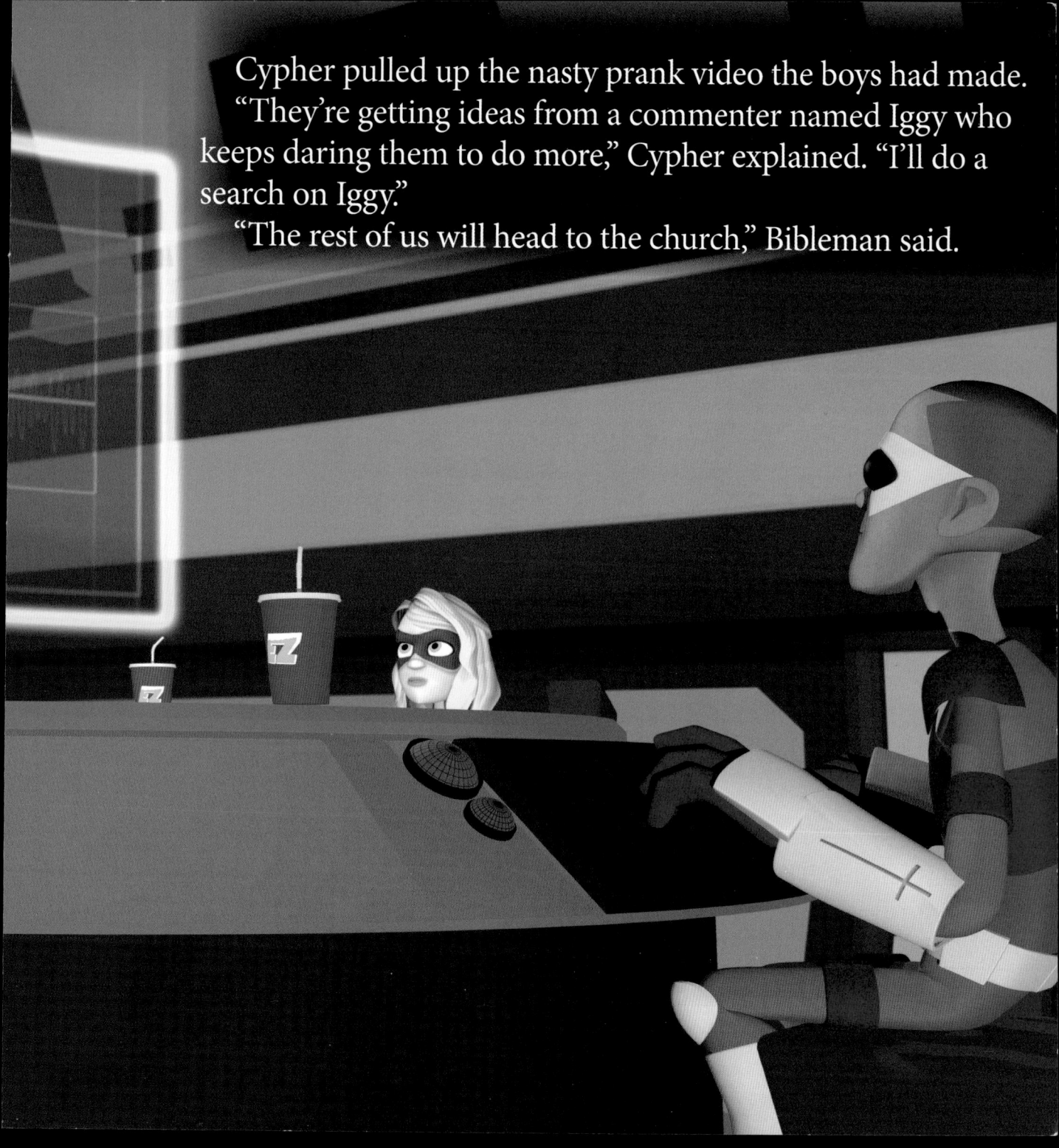

Cypher pulled up the nasty prank video the boys had made. "They're getting ideas from a commenter named Iggy who keeps daring them to do more," Cypher explained. "I'll do a search on Iggy."

"The rest of us will head to the church," Bibleman said.

At headquarters, the Bibleteam received a message from Pastor Roberts: "Bibleman, I've discovered that some of our youth members have been playing mean pranks on elderly people. We would be blessed if you could come meet with the kids."

Storylines by Wayne Zeitner

Adaptations by Caroline Slemp

Printed in the United States of America.

ISBN: 978-1-4336-4941-7

Published by B&H Publishing Group Nashville, Tennessee

Unless otherwise noted, all Scripture quotations are taken from the Christian Standard Bible®, Copyright © 2017 by Holman Bible Publishers. Used by permission. Christian Standard Bible® and CSB® are federally registered trademarks of Holman Bible Publishers.

Printed in LongGang District, Shenzhen, China, November 2016

1 2 3 4 5   21 20 19 18 17

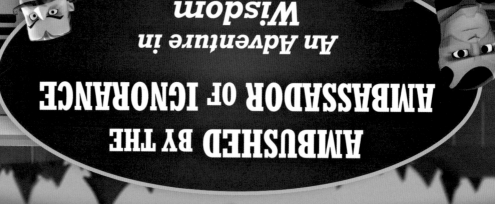